WHY DOES SANTA CELEBRATE CHRISTMAS?

BY CHERYL FOOTE GIMBEL
ILLUSTRATED BY WENDELIN MANERS

JP

JALMAR PRESS
ROLLING HILLS ESTATES, CALIFORNIA

Gimbel, Cheryl Foote, 1939-
    Why does Santa celebrate Christmas?

    Summary: Recounts how a toymaker at the North Pole
heard of the birth of Jesus and began the custom of
sharing each year as a celebration of the event.
    1. Santa Claus—Juvenile fiction.   2. Jesus Christ—
Juvenile fiction.   [1. Santa Claus—Fiction.   2. Jesus
Christ—Nativity—Fiction.   3. Christmas—Fiction.
4. Stories in rhyme] I. Maners, Wendelin, ill.
II. Title.
PZ8.3.G4235Wh   1990   [E]   90-4222
ISBN 0-915190-67-2

Published by Jalmar Press
45 Hitching Post Drive
Rolling Hills Estates, California 90274
Tel: (310) 784-0016

First edition
Printing 10 9 8 7 6 5 4 3 2

Printed in Hong Kong

DEDICATION

This book is dedicated to our mom
and grandma, Marjorie Foote,
whose love and persuasion
convinced us to share our story
with children of all ages.

Mommy,
why does Santa Claus bring me presents
on Jesus' birthday?

S it down my child and listen to me,
to a story of Christmas and a tannenbaum tree;

about angels and elves and a star in the sky,
about Santa and reindeer and the reasons why.

'T was a child who was born on this very day,
in a manger at Bethlehem, on a bed of hay.

To Mary and Joseph was this child born,
a gift to the world on this very morn.

Now there was in the sky a special star,
and wise men and shepherds came traveling afar,

to see what the angels had whispered to them
about Jesus, the child, a king among men.

With gold and frankincense and myrrh they rode;
on camels and mules they brought their great load.

The gifts they had chosen were fit for a king,
and for little Lord Jesus the heavens did sing.

And angels carried across the earth,
with songs in their hearts, the news of his birth.

Across the world where the winds did blow,
the news was soon spread to a man we all know.

'T was a funny old toymaker at the snowy North Pole,
his name, Santa Claus, a jolly old soul.

Now he and his wife had lived all alone,
without a child of their very own.

Their prayers were answered this wonderful morn,
for angels told them that this day had been born,

a child for them to cherish and love,
a child of God from the heavens above.

Their joy was so great that they readied their sleigh,
to go to the forest where the elves did play.
They spoke to the elves and the animals there,
and asked each one to kneel with a prayer.

And when the trees heard their prayers that sweet night,
they asked old Santa Claus if they too, could bring light.

S o Santa and elves and reindeer and all
of the forest's animals — some large and some small,
lit candles to Jesus so the world would all see,
and placed them on branches of the finest green tree.

And thus, his first Christmas, Santa did share
with his friends in the forest and all who lived there.

And so, little one, was the first Christmas day
when all of God's creatures did kneel and did pray.

Now listen dear child for the carolers' voices
each Christmas day, as the whole world rejoices.

F or Santa, the toymaker, did love Jesus so dearly,
that each Christmas day he celebrates yearly
by giving to all good girls and good boys,
beautiful presents and wonderful toys,

as he and his reindeer circle the earth,
to celebrate Christmas and Jesus' birth.

ABOUT THE AUTHOR

Cheryl Foote Gimbel was raised in San Marino, California, and attended the University of Southern California where she majored in music and fine arts. The author has always loved working with children and co-founded Peninsula Children's Theater in 1972 in Palos Verdes, California, where she continues to volunteer. Cheryl enjoys traveling, interior design, and ballroom dancing. Writing is one of Cheryl's hobbies, so it was quite natural for her to work with her daughter to create this charming Christmas fantasy book.

ABOUT THE ILLUSTRATOR

Wendelin Maners lives in Manhattan Beach, California, a short distance from her mother. She studied art at the University of Puget Sound and graduated from the University of Southern California with a degree in business. Wendelin finds that she can relax after a hectic day by listening to her favorite classical music and painting. Her gentle watercolors are enjoyed by many people. Although a published illustrator, this is her first children's book. Wendelin is an active volunteer in her church and also enjoys skiing, tennis, body surfing, and bicycling.